HAPPY

DREAMER

 W9-BVD-673

This book is a work of fiction. Names, characters, places, and incidents are either the product of the author's imagination or are used fictitiously, and any resemblance to actual persons, living or dead, business establishments, events, or locales is entirely coincidental.

No part of this publication may be reproduced, stored in a retrieval system, or transmitted in any form or by any means, electronic, mechanical, photocopying, recording, or otherwise, without written permission of the publisher. For information regarding permission, write to Orchard Books, Scholastic Inc., Attention: Permissions Department, 557 Broadway, New York, NY 10012.

ISBN 978-1-338-54604-0

Copyright © 2017 by Peter H. Reynolds. All rights reserved. Published by Orchard Books, an imprint of Scholastic Inc., *Publishers since 1920.* ORCHARD BOOKS and design are registered trademarks of Watts Publishing Group, Ltd., used under license. SCHOLASTIC and associated logos are trademarks and/or registered trademarks of Scholastic Inc.

The publisher does not have any control over and does not assume any responsibility for author or third-party websites or their content.

12 11 10 9 8 7 6 5 4 3 2 1   19 20 21 22 23 24

Printed in the U.S.A.   88

This edition first printing, January 2019

The text type and display type are hand lettered by Peter H. Reynolds.

Reynolds Studio assistance by Julia Anne Young

Book design by Patti Ann Harris

HAPPY
DREAMER
by PETER H. REYNOLDS

SCHOLASTIC INC.

I AM A HAPPY
DREAMER.
I'm really good at
dreaming.
DAY DREAMS.
BIG DREAMS.
Little dreams.
CREATIVE DREAMS.

dreamer maximus!

But my dreams have
a mind of their own.

SOMETIMES MY MIND JUST TAKES FLIGHT! I HEAR A **BEAT** AND I GOTTA MOVE...

THEN I HEAR ANOTHER AND ANOTHER!

WISH YOU COULD

HEAR

INSIDE MY HEAD

TRUMPETY, ZIGZAG JAZZ!

when I make time
to stay still and
hear myself think—
to let go and see
what takes shape.

DO YOU SEE THAT?

Sometimes I'm a swing-high dreamer... WAY UP HIGH...BEYOND THE CLOUDS...

SO HIGH I CAN TOUCH THE SKY!

I can also be a **LOUD** dreamer!

HELLO,

WORLD!

I'M A SHOUT-AT-THE-TOP-OF-MY-LUNGS DREAMER!

(EVEN IF I'M JUST A LOUD-INSIDE-MY-HEAD DREAMER!)

SOMETIMES...

I'M A COLORFUL DREAMER,

PAINTING MY OWN PATH
FULL OF SURPRISES AT EVERY TURN.

I can dream
even when the
lights are **OUT**.

ALL CIRCUITS ON!
FIREWORKS!
I LIGHT UP!
I'M ALL EARS,
EYES, HEART, AND MIND!

Cleaning up hides my treasures.

If YOU MAKE ME,
I will put my things away.
But then there is
less ME to show.

These are the moments
I feel alone.

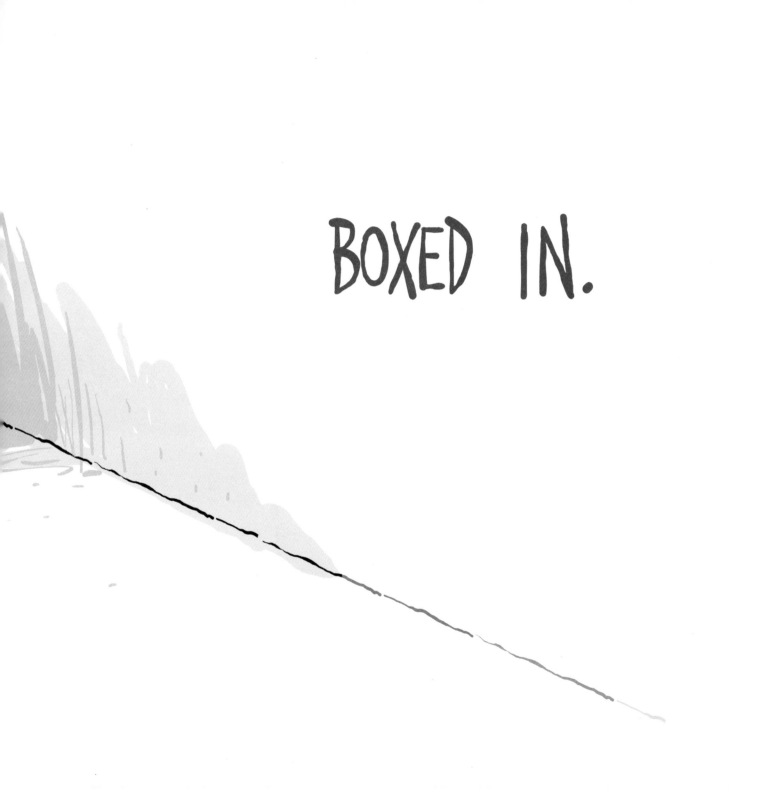

And yet, I always find a way back.

Plunging into amazing, delightful, happy dreams.

I'm really good at being me.

A DREAMER

SURPRISING

CARING

FUNNY

GENTLE

SMART

And when I
TUMBLE
back to earth...

Dreamers have a way of bouncing back...

AND MOVING FORWARD!

WINGED DREAMER

ROYAL DREAMER

THINKING DREAMER

SWEET DREAMER

SUNNY DREAMER

FLOATING DREAMER

LOVE DREAMER

WILD DREAMER

CRAZY DREAMER

POWER DREAMER

CIVIC DREAMER

SECRET DREAMER

ICE CREAM HAPPY

SUNSHINE HAPPY

MAKE A DIFFERENCE HAPPY

NAP HAPPY

MUSIC HAPPY

DANCE HAPPY

PEACEFUL HAPPY

CATCH HAPPY

KINDNESS HAPPY

AWE HAPPY

SILLY HAPPY

FOOT-STOMPIN' HAPPY

THERE ARE SO MANY
WAYS TO BE A

HAPPY
DREAMER!

(WHAT KIND OF DREAMER ARE YOU?)

DREAMY DREAMER

TEAM DREAMER

VISION DREAMER

GOAL DREAMER

STAGE DREAMER

STELLAR DREAMER

NIGHT DREAMER

DAY DREAMER

BIG DREAMER

SPACE DREAMER

FIERCE DREAMER

GIANT DREAMER

But the best way
to be a happy dreamer?

Just BE YOU.

Which is why this book is dedicated to you. YES, YOU!

HAPPY DREAMER

I'm a dreamer.
Always have been.
Not all grown-ups
were happy with my
dreaming—my
zigzaggy brain—
but I was lucky
some were. And
my parents, well,
they let me be me—
loved me— and
things worked out
pretty well.
—Peter

PETER HAMILTON REYNOLDS

Peter H. Reynolds is a *New York Times*–
bestselling author and illustrator of many books for
children, including *The Word Collector*, *The Dot*, and
The North Star. His books have been translated into
over twenty-five languages around the globe and are
celebrated worldwide. In 1996, he founded FableVision
with his brother, Paul, as a social change agency to
help move the world to a better place by creating
"stories that matter, stories that move."
He lives in Dedham, Massachusetts, with his family.
Visit him online at peterhreynolds.com.